WHAT'S NEW?

by John Ryckman   Illustrated by Mark Craig

John McInnes, *Senior Author*   Glen Dixon   John Ryckman

EARLY BIRD COLLECTION AUTHORS

PUBLISHED SIMULTANEOUSLY IN 1990 BY:

Nelson Canada,
A Division of International
Thomson Limited
1120 Birchmount Road
Scarborough, Ontario   M1K 5G4

AND

Delmar Publishers Inc.,
A Division of Thomson Corp.
2 Computer Drive, West
Box 15015
Albany, NY 12212-5015

**Canadian Cataloguing
in Publication Data**

Ryckman, John
What's new?

(Early bird collection)
ISBN 0-17-603029-8

I. Craig, Mark.   II. Title.   III. Series.

PS8585.Y35W53 1990   jC813'.54   C89-090546-0
PZ7.R83Wh 1990

**Library of Congress
Cataloging-in-Publication Data**

Ryckman, John
What's New?

(Early bird)
  Summary: Mom, Dad, and the kids have a birthday for a
special member of the family.
  [1. Parties—fiction. 2. Birthdays—Fiction. 3. Dogs—
Fiction] I. Title. II. Series. Early bird (Albany, N.Y.)
PZ7.R9588Wh   1989   [E]   89-23567
ISBN 0-8273-4126-1

© Nelson Canada,
A Division of International Thomson Limited, 1990

Co-ordinating Editor: Jean Stinson
Project Manager: Jocelyn Van Huyse-Wilson
Editor: Irene Cox
Art Director: Lorraine Tuson
Series Design and Art Direction: Rob McPhail
Photography: Jeremy Jones Photography
Typesetting: Trigraph Inc.

1 2 3 4 5 6 7 8 9 0   EB   9 8 7 6 5 4 3 2 1 0